BORDERTOWNS

Photographs by
Marc Gaede

Edited by
Marnie Walker Gaede

CHACO PRESS / LA CAÑADA, CALIFORNIA

FOR LIFE, FOR HOPE

without malice
without judgement

Copyright 1988 © by Chaco Press

All rights reserved. No part of this publication may be
reproduced or transmitted in any form (except short quotes
for the purpose of review) without prior permission of the publisher.

ISBN 0-9616019-2-2.

Library of Congress Catalog Card Number 87-72564.

Composed and printed in the United States of America.

FIRST EDITION.

BORDERTOWNS

1. *Passed out in Winslow*

Prologue

I REMEMBER IT WAS A LATE WINTER NIGHT and I was walking through the Hopi village of Hotevilla. All traces of winter's snow had gone but the cold wind remained to blow sand among the stone houses. The windows cast an orange madder glow given by lanterns hung from beamed ceilings. Walking on the sandy road, my thoughts were interrupted by a faint sound that became more pronounced as I distinguished between the wind and what became a human cry.

Moving closer in the darkness, I made out a cluster of houses in whose shadows a person was in grief. Suddenly a passing car flashed its lights, revealing in a closed doorway a man being supported by a woman from behind with her arms around his chest. Quickly the lights were gone, but his sound of despair remained. The cry was far beyond that of tears — a steady flow of total and infinite pain. The cry was flowing on the wind, through the streets, around the houses, entering windows, doors and through the rock walls themselves.

The village was one and the people sat quietly at their tables, walked softly in the rooms and the children intuitively remained unnoticed. Even the normally ever-present village dogs were nowhere to be seen as the insidious wail rose to crush all objects before it. It was as if the rocks, trees and the very night itself also felt the torment and politely acquiesced in this declaration of death. Later I was to learn someone had died in the vast void called the borderlands.

2. *Pete, Gallup*

3. *Gallup*

4. *Gallup*

5. *Holbrook, Arizona*

6. *Winslow*

7. *Sammy, Gallup*

8. *Joey, Gallup*

9. *Joey, Gallup*

10. *Two kids, Gallup*

11. *Jigger with her children, Winslow*

13. *Black hat, Gallup*

12. *Ray, Gallup*

11. *Michael Tom and Taylor Todachinic, Gallup*

16. Gary Charley, Moenkopi, 1981

15. Gary Charley, Flagstaff, 1980

17. *Gary Charley frozen in ice, Farmington, 1981*

18. *Gary Charley's tombstone, Bita Hochee*

19. Holbrook

20. *Gallup*

21. *Gallup, New Mexico*

22. *After school drink, Holbrook*

23. *Winslow*

24. *Holbrook*

25. *Gray Mountain*

26. *Gray Mountain, Arizona*

27. *Housing, Mexican Hat*

28. *Mexican Hat, Utah*

29. *Graffiti, Fort Defiance*

30. *Graffiti, Fort Defiance*

31. *Rodeo, Gallup*

32. *Rodeo crowd, Gallup*

34. *Barrel racing, Gallup*

33. *Bull dogging, Gallup*

35. *Behind the chutes, Gallup*

36. *Behind the chutes, Gallup*

37. *Behind the bar, Holbrook*

39. *Prairie Moon ladies, Winslow*

38. *Prairie Moon lady, Winslow*

40. *Jasper, Proprietor, Prairie Moon Tavern, Winslow*

41. *Palomino Bar, Gallup*

42. *Jerry Franklin and the Navajo Midnighters, Milan's Club, Gallup*

44. Rosetree Bar, Flagstaff

43. Milan's Club, Gallup

45. *Inside the Commercial Club, Gallup*

46. *Inside the American Bar, Gallup*

47. *Farmington, New Mexico*

48. Holbrook

49. *Air fresheners, Gallup*

50. *Stealing his boots, Flagstaff*

52. *Passed out in the truck, Gallup*

51. *Tall ones for the road, Gallup*

53. *"Hey guys, come over here," Winslow*

54. *But he likes to sleep there, Gallup*

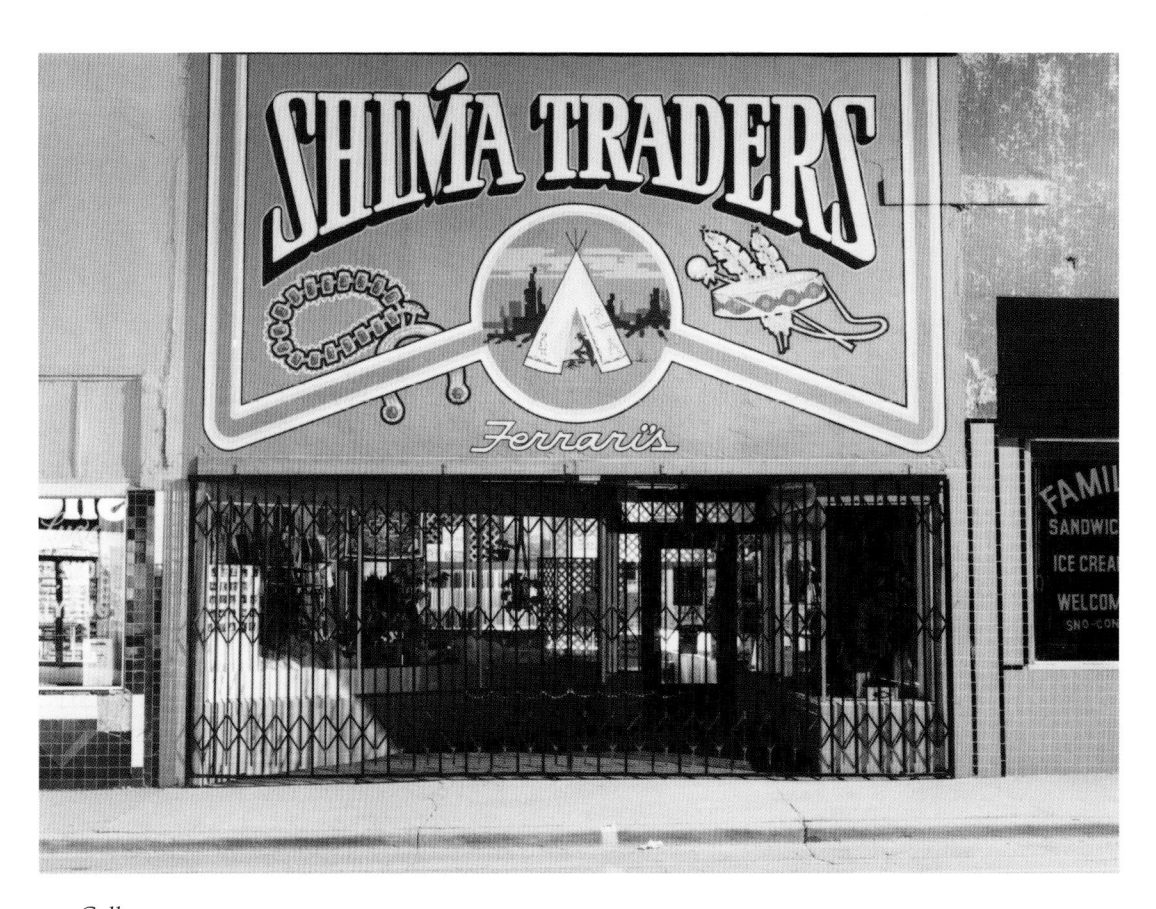

55. *Gallup*

56. *Gallup*

57. *Gallup*

58. *Gallup*

59. *Cut them out, Holbrook*

60. *Wrong way on the freeway, near Fort Wingate*

61. *Wrong way on the highway, Gallup*

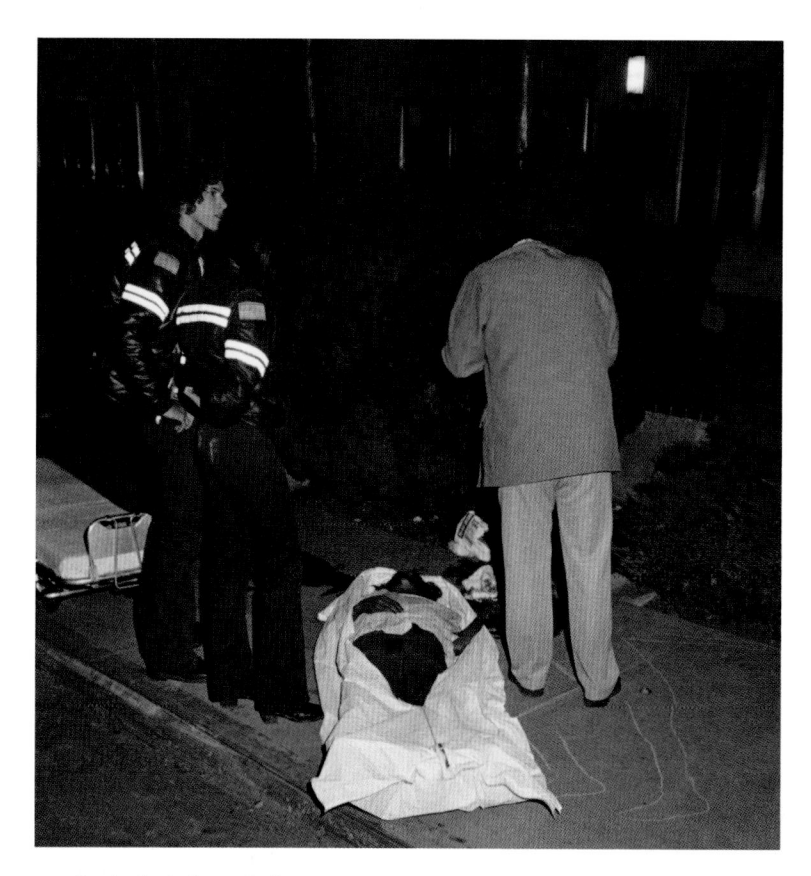

63. *In the body bag, Gallup*

62. *Run over by a drunk, Gallup*

64. *Run over by a train, Flagstaff*

65. *They cannot save the baby, Farmington*

66. *Hit the car head on, Gray Mountain*

67. *The little girl is gone, Gray Mountain*

68. *Body outline, blood and a quarter, Gray Mountain*

69. *Looking for trouble, Gallup*

70. *Randy, Gallup*

71. *He wears a top hat, Gallup*

72. *Waiting, Gallup*

73. *"No pictures, no pictures!" Gallup*

74. *"Tell us what happened,"* Gallup

75. *Donna, Gallup*

76. *Inspection day, Gallup*

77. *Time to get out, Gallup*

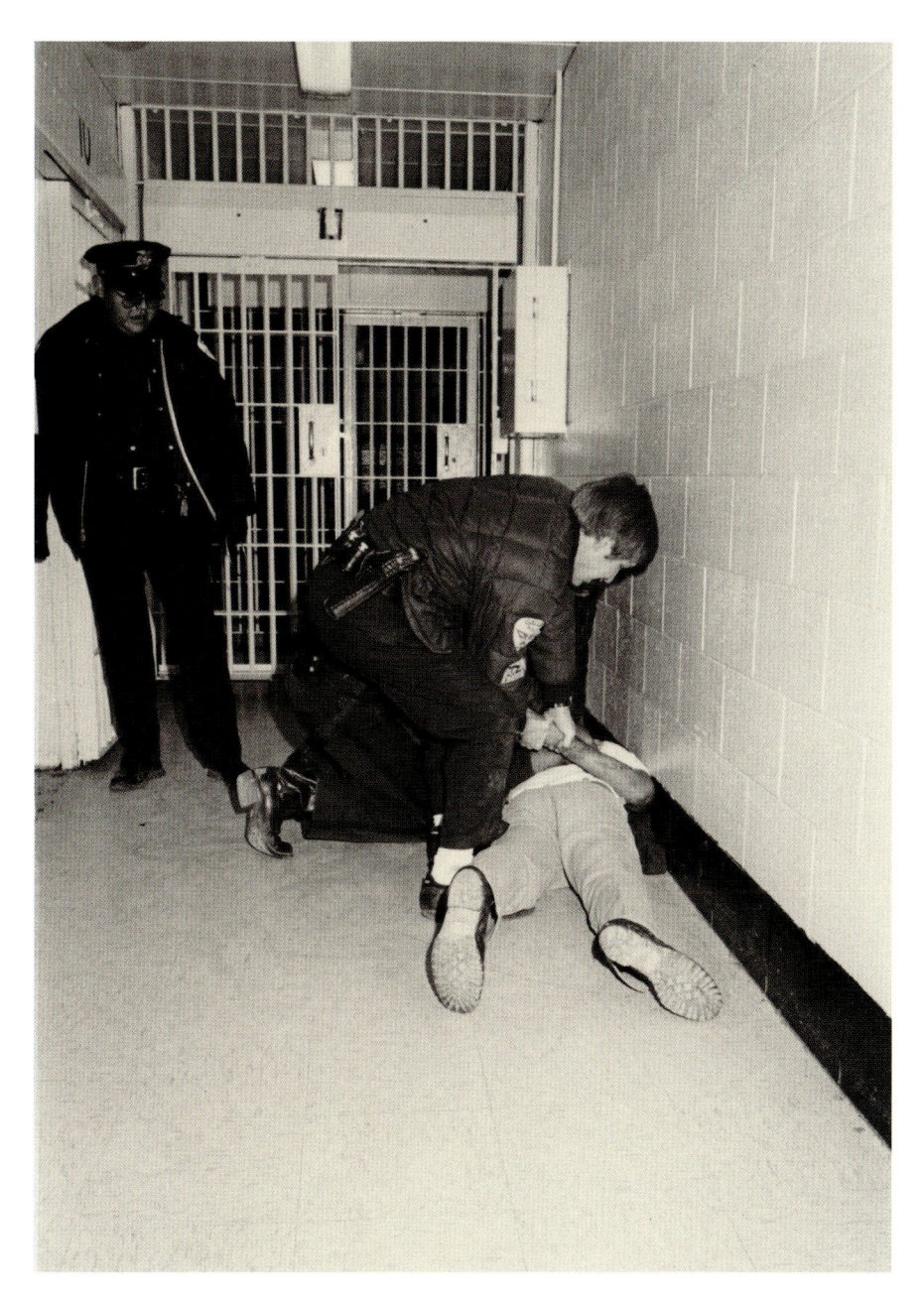

78. *"Like hell you'll get me in that cell!" Gallup*

80. *In the side pocket, Gallup*

79. *He is trying to pick the lock, Gallup*

81. *The small tank, Gallup*

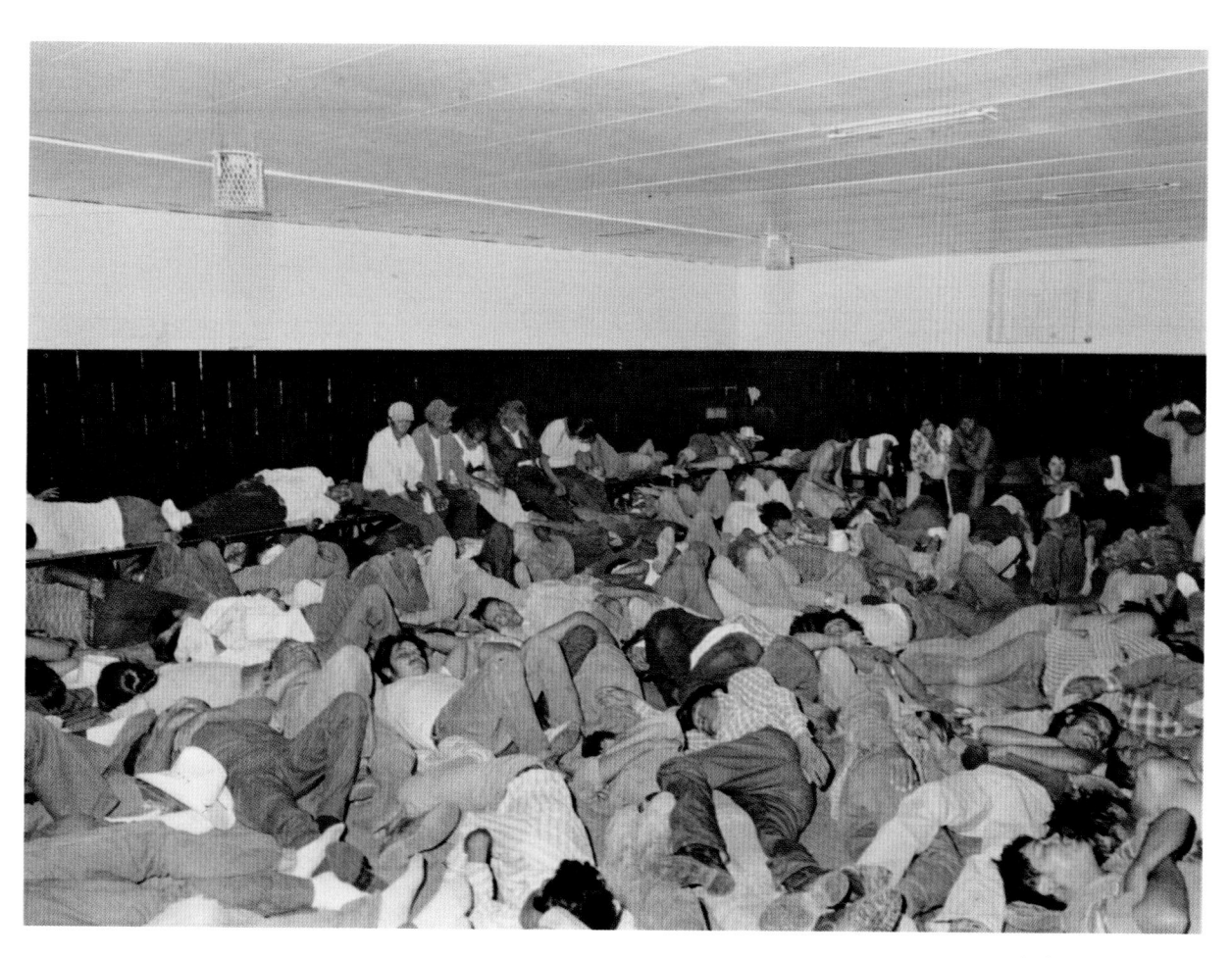

82. *The big tank, Gallup*

83. *Fight! Gallup*

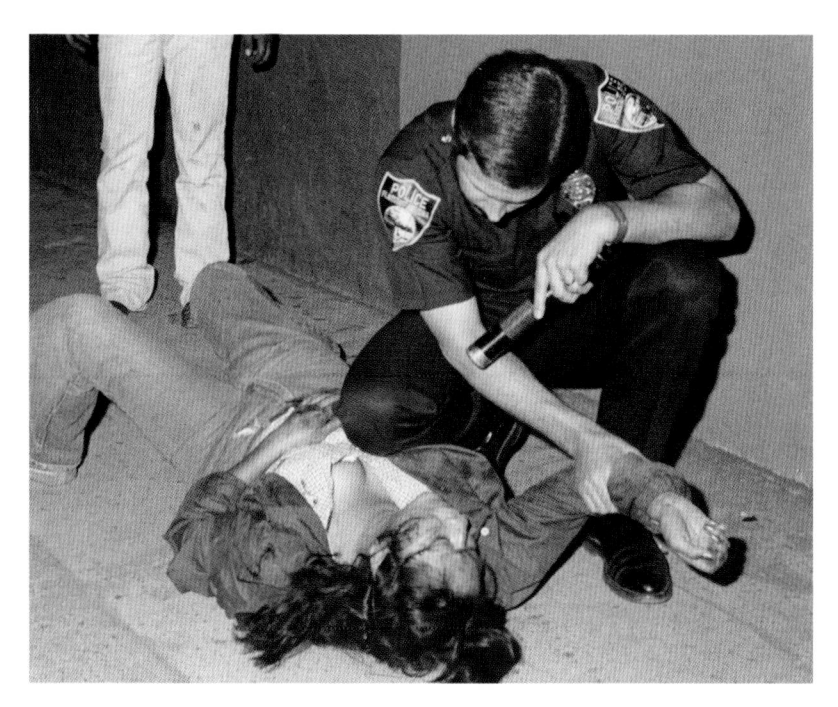

84. *Checking her eyes, Flagstaff*

85. *Hit in the face with a pool cue, Club 66, Flagstaff*

86. *He just shakes, Gallup*

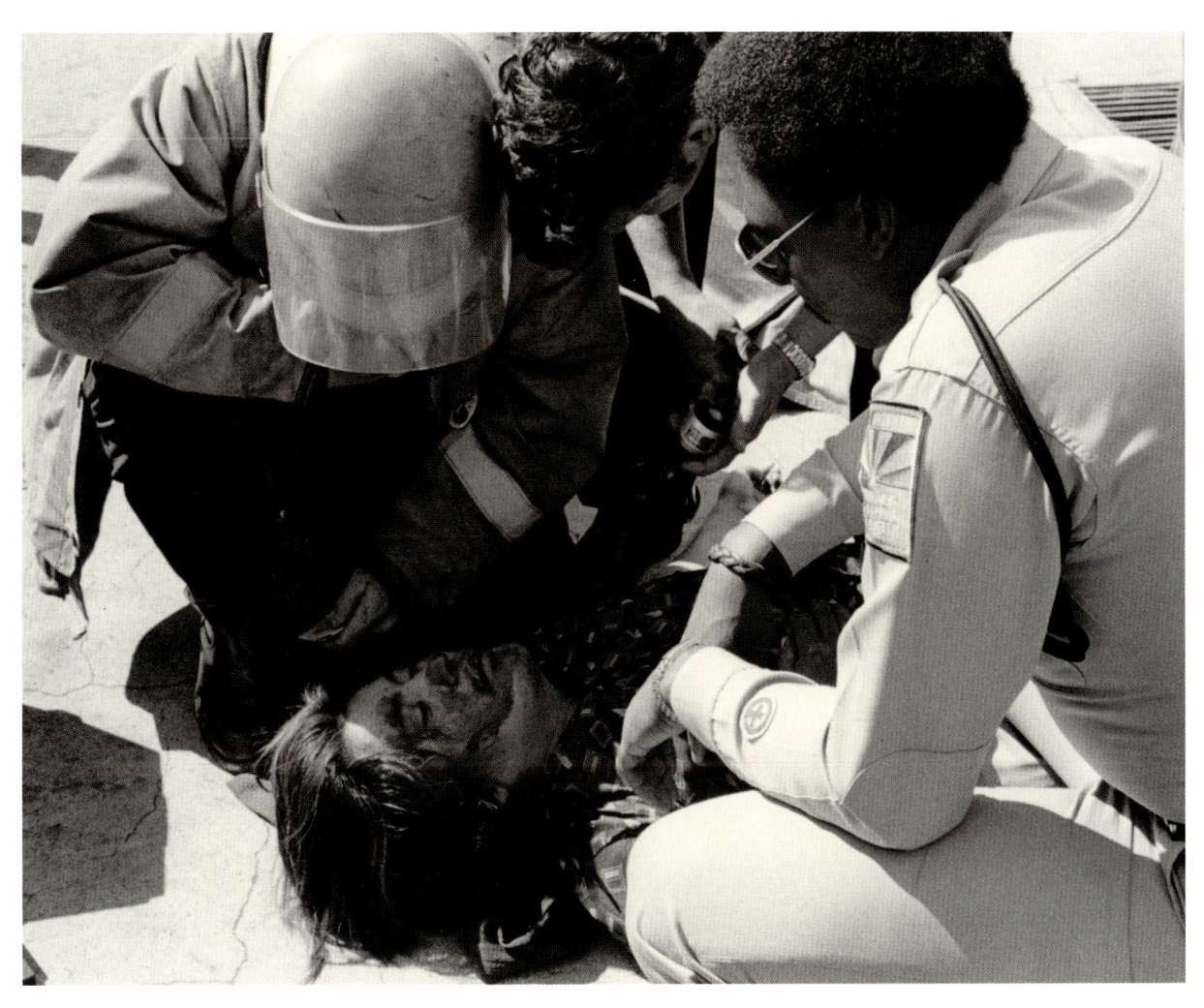

87. *Dying words, Flagstaff*

88. *Stabbed in the chest, Gallup*

89. *Slashed across the face, Commercial Club, Gallup*

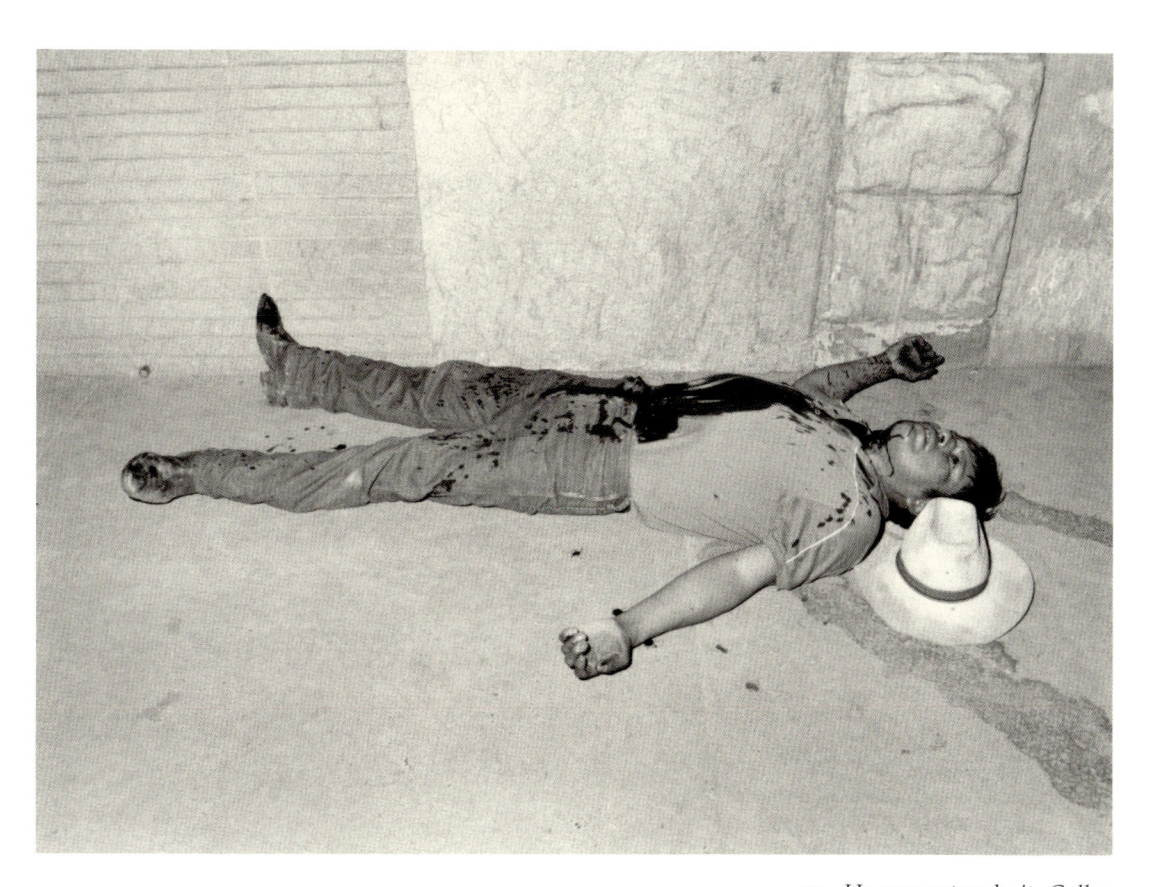

90. *He may not make it*, Gallup

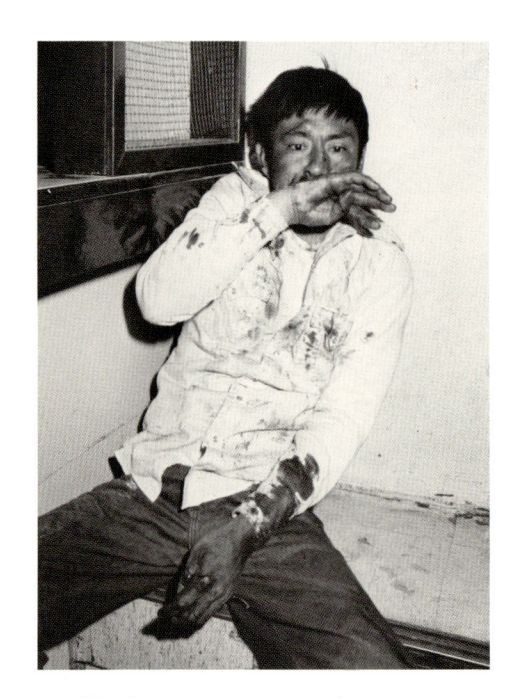

92. "And my money too," Gallup

91. "They took my money," Gallup

93. *"They took everything I had," Gallup*

94. *"They cleaned me out," Gallup*

95. *He is going to jump, Indian Hospital, Gallup*

96. *"One step closer and I'll jump!" Indian Hospital, Gallup*

97. *Veteran's Cemetery, Window Rock*

98. *El Presidente, looking, Gallup*

Image Notes

8. & 9. *Joey*
    The police say that Joey had a brain operation long ago. He is only marginally able to maintain a grasp of reality. They also say he gets worse each year.

11. *Jigger with her children*
    Jigger did not have a resident husband which made it difficult for her to feed and care for her five children. She lives on the west end of town, and can be seen pulling her children in the wagon on daily errands.

12. *Ray*
    Ray dresses up for downtown Gallup on Sundays even though the bars are closed and the girls are gone.

14. *Michael Tom and Taylor Todachinie*
    They both have degenerative, terminal diseases. Michael's is more advanced so Taylor pushes the wheelchair. At night in Gallup, they can be heard cruising through the darkness by announcing their presence with the aid of Michael's ghetto blaster — which fades as they disappear into the night. Taylor has to protect Michael since he was the object of cruel attention by some of the local children. Once he was set on fire, and on another time the police report finding him stuck with home made darts. Michael enjoys an occasional benevolent police

car ride and keeps photographs of his favorite policemen on his bedroom wall.

15. 16.   *Gary Charley*
&
17. 18. Gary Charley could have been an outstanding Indian artist. He could draw a complex scene in seconds with a natural grace and beauty. That Gary died before his gift of talent could be developed is a fate common among young Indians.

21. *Gallup, New Mexico*
Few would dispute Gallup's claim to be the "largest Indian trading center in the world." Liquor is illegal on most of the surrounding Indian reservations whose people come to Gallup when they want to drink something other than expensive bootleg wine. A major portion of the town's commerce is the liquor industry, consequently Gallup can be a wild town with drunks everywhere. Car accidents are commonplace. It is this impression which creates Gallup's image, not the fact that it is located in beautiful surroundings of alpine forests, high plateaus and magnificent canyons.

22. *After school drink*
He was there in the late afternoon, passed out and sitting on his school books, with his empty bottle respectfully placed in the doorway.

38. 39.   *Prairie Moon Tavern*
&
40. The Prairie Moon Tavern in Winslow, Arizona is a friendly place. Patrons of diverse ethnic backgrounds drink, dance and make merry into the late hours of the night. Prairie Moon ladies are noted for their good looks, gentle affection and unusual attentiveness.

51. *Tall ones for the road*
In the bordertowns, it is not uncommon for everyone to run from an accident scene, regardless of who is at fault, because the participants have all been drinking. One time there was an accident in Gallup involving six vehicles, all of which were abandoned by the time the police arrived. In this instance, when the guilty parties took off, they, uncustomarily, left the beer behind.

54. *But he likes to sleep there*
On cold nights it is not unusual for drunks to sleep under cars for warmth. This works fine unless the car drives off leaving crumpled bodies behind. Police in the bordertowns know to look under vehicles for people. One night in Gallup, a man became entangled beneath a tanker truck after he had crawled under it for shelter. He was dragged thirty-five miles, and body parts were scattered along the way. Police cars drove four abreast from Gallup to Window Rock picking up the pieces.

59. *Cut them out*
The children were trapped in the crushed car. The Fire Department was called in to remove them with the jaws-of-life. The rescuers knew they were dead, but continued their work. "No pictures," yelled the crowd. Tensions were high and the frustration of watching the agonizingly slow life-saving effort suddenly became directed at the photographer. One young tough jumped out, ready for fight, and the spectators were with him. The moment was abated by a patrolman, who appeared with his nightstick and drove them back.

The other driver was a big man whose pickup, equipped with balloon tires, made him feel more powerful as he cruised down Holbrook's main drag. The excess of inflated strength, however, was also proportionate to a loss of maneuverability and stopping power due to the oversized tires. When the small economy car containing a young mother and her children turned in front of the pickup, the brakes, designed for tires one quarter the size, were of little use to prevent the collision, and the truck crushed the small car. After the victims had been removed, he strolled over to a patrolman and asked if the children had been badly hurt. When told they were both dead his big legs suddenly gave way and two hundred pounds came crashing to the ground. Yelling disclaimers and bargains to God, he thrashed the asphalt.

62. & 63. *Run over by a drunk*
The young cowboy and his partner were walking down the street carrying their bronc riding gear and talking about the

day's events at the Ceremonial Rodeo. Earlier, two women had picked up some men to go drinking with, and one of those men had taken command of the car. Approaching an intersection of downtown Gallup, they decided to change directions. The driver attempted a hard left turn with too much speed, aided by too much drink. The car hurtled over the curb and into the walking bronc riders. One was knocked clear, but the cowboy was under the car, alive, as it came to a stop. Alive, that is, until the driver decided to make his escape by backing up into the street, crushing the cowboy's skull. The police later found the car parked at Milan's Club and the suspects dancing inside.

68. *Body outline, blood and a quarter*
Body outlines are a standard procedure in all fatal investigations. This one remained visible on the highway for months after the accident until the victim's family came from their village and blackened it with paint. However, it still can be seen, in the right light, on the first curve above Gray Mountain.

73. *"No pictures, no pictures!"*
For years she has walked the streets of Gallup. A small man usually accompanies her and they sort trash bins together for a living. Her face is a mask, but in the one good eye something of the woman can be seen. Perhaps she isn't as old as the first impression portrays. When the photographer previously requested photographs, she would always respond, "no pictures, no pictures!" But this time she gave in, probably for the little money offered.

76. *Inspection day, Gallup Police*
That the Gallup Police are tough goes without saying. It was commonly known by other police departments, if you could last in Gallup, you could work on just about any police force in this country. One time the director of L.A.'s Special Urban Task Force happened to watch two Gallup cops take down six suspects, one by a hurled night stick. He approached them passing out his card saying, "boys, if you ever need a job..."

82. *The big tank*
With dimensions of 4,500 square feet, *Police Magazine*, reports it to be the largest jail cell in the United States. It holds 500 people...uncomfortably. The heat generated by so many bodies creates a furnace effect, and there is a blast of hot air on approach to the entrance. At first glance, this image usually provokes accusations of injustice. But those interned here will go home to their families the following day. Without protective custody, there would be an endless nightly series of beatings, stabbings, muggings, rapes, deaths by exposure and car accidents.

88. *Stabbed in the chest*
During a fight among friends a knife suddenly appeared in an emotional moment. His girlfriend is holding the wounds closed from behind with a towel. His eyes indicate he is in shock. Later, it was said that the girlfriend had cut him. Or was it his brother?

89. *Slashed across the face*
A report came in indicating a knife fight with injuries. At the back of the bar near the dance floor the victim was found. He had been slashed across the face with a razor and blood poured to the floor. When the police came to take him away, he suddenly stood and gulped down his beer in a last minute show of machismo. Once outside, he had to be restrained while a compress was applied. The blood loss was massive and he went into convulsions before the ambulance arrived.

97. *Veteran's Cemetery, Window Rock*
This is sacred ground to the Navajos. To serve in the Armed Services represents a special honor to most American Indians. A quick tour of the tombstone inscriptions reveals that a remarkably high number of the veterans died before they turned forty. These epitaphs testify to a tragic pattern of early death among the Navajo.

98. *El Presidente, looking*
El Presidente is the name he goes by. It is said he was a POW tortured senseless by the Japanese in World War II, and he has been mentally disturbed ever since. A chronic insomniac, El Presidente always comes out after the bars are closed at 2 A.M. and wanders about in his make-shift uniform looking with his flashlight. No one knows what he is looking for and he never seems to find anything. He just looks, and looks and looks.

Afterword

THE SEEDS FOR THIS BOOK BEGAN when, as a child, I was witness to the adversity within the bordertowns. Because it is illegal to sell liquor on most southwestern reservations, resident Indians who want to drink visit the surrounding communities. These bordertowns have the liquor and are settings of varied and extensive drinking activities. The fact most Indians have neither shelter nor money for rooms makes the display of binge drinking visible to everyone. Defenseless, these individuals are made objects of violence and degradation by their own people and by other ethnic groups.

Teenagers, where I grew up, made sport in roughing up the drunks and stealing their hats. During the early 1970's, in Farmington, New Mexico, a group of white juveniles formed a club where membership was contingent upon participating in the murder of a drunk Indian and cutting off a trophy finger. Until recently, all bordertowns exhibited an insensitive callousness toward the visiting, alcoholic Indian.

I first grasped this disparity vividly when, as a fourteen-year-old, I was picked up by the Flagstaff police for underage drinking with seven Indian companions. All seven were given two months jail time if they were over eighteen years old, probation if they were under. I was released to my older sister without charge. The eight of us who shared that fateful bottle of rum have remained good friends over the years, but I have shouldered a burden for that event. They have accepted it as a fact of life — a small reality in a world which provides far more terrifying encounters with prejudice.

The decision to do a photographic book on the Indian bordertowns came suddenly one evening in Gallup, New Mexico. My wife and I had made it an annual event to attend the Zuni Shalako ceremony, and one year we decided to walk around nearby Gallup before the festivities. As we approached the Chief Theater, two Indian youth gangs came together with belts in their hands and the buckles swinging in the air. The fight lasted only a few seconds, but the sharpened buckles had done their damage by leaving several individuals badly cut. Cars rapidly pulled up to the scene, the young men quickly loaded their wounded and took off. Two police officers on foot patrol arrived within minutes, but all that remained were pools of blood and eye witness accounts. My camera was in the car a few blocks away and I regretted the lost opportunity for an unusual image. I was determined to get the next one.

In 1980 I opened an Indian art store in downtown Flagstaff near the front street bars. There I found interesting people and dramatic events almost commonplace. My business made it necessary to visit other bordertowns to purchase arts and crafts. I took along my camera. With nothing to do after a day of trading, I walked the streets looking for more subjects. Later I carried a police radio to follow the action, and was often the first to arrive upon a scene. Towards the end of the seven-year span covered in the project, I spent most of my effort riding with the police in Arizona and New Mexico. This allowed photography in situations impossible by other means.

All of the portraits reproduced in this book were taken with the permission of the subjects, most of whom were paid. The portraits were never forced or exposed clandestinely. All of the newsworthy images were taken spontaneously without permission as permitted by law. Some of the locations have been changed and some of the faces retouched to protect innocent people. Although this is not required legally, it is not the intention of this book to hurt anyone. There is pain enough presented in some of these images, and every effort has been taken to not create more.

The only picture I didn't take is the Gary Charley death image. It was made by the Medical Investigator of San Juan County and released by the State of New Mexico Medical Examiner's Office. The family of Gary Charley made the decision to grant a release in hope that other young Indian people might gain wisdom from Gary's misfortune.

It is the purpose of this book to present a situation that needs to be recognized as a reality and a problem. I tried to avoid sheer horror, and most of the excessively shocking images were excluded or taken from a distance. To those who see their family and friends on these pages, please forgive me. Their pain and tragedy are in my memory forever. Hardly a day goes by that these people do not cross my mind, and in a sense, I have scarred myself with this book. But, I know in the long run, far more good will come from it than harm.

In what is probably one of the greatest novels ever written on the American Indian, James Welch's *Fools Crow*, Fools Crow has the final vision for his people's fate. "He saw white children playing and laughing in a world the Indian had possessed. And he saw the Indian children, quiet and huddled together, alone and foreign in their own country." Had Fools Crow's vision been stronger he might have seen distant towns surrounding Indian land. Towns on the plains, in the desert, against the mountains, where Indians fight in the streets, lay drunk in the alleys, families torn to shreds and heritage forgotten. The faces and the words echo the past, and hope of a different vision waits in the shadows.

List of Photographs

1. Passed out in Winslow, 1980
2. Pete, Gallup, 1986
3. Gallup, 1987
4. Gallup, 1982
5. Holbrook, Arizona, 1982
6. Winslow, 1980
7. Sammy, Gallup, 1986
8. Joey, Gallup, 1986
9. Joey, Gallup, 1986
10. Two kids, Gallup, 1986
11. Jigger with her children, Winslow, 1982
12. Ray, Gallup, 1986
13. Black hat, Gallup, 1986
14. Michael Tom and Taylor Todachinie, Gallup, 1986
15. Gary Charley, Flagstaff, 1980
16. Gary Charley, Moenkopi, 1981
17. Gary Charley frozen in ice, Farmington, 1981
18. Gary Charley's tombstone, Bita Hochee, 1982
19. Holbrook, 1984
20. Gallup, 1980
21. Gallup, New Mexico, 1980
22. After school drink, Holbrook, 1980
23. Winslow, 1985
24. Holbrook, 1981

25. Gray Mountain, 1981
26. Gray Mountain, Arizona, 1980
27. Housing, Mexican Hat, 1981
28. Mexican Hat, Utah, 1982
29. Graffiti, Fort Defiance, 1981
30. Graffiti, Fort Defiance, 1981
31. Rodeo, Gallup, 1981
32. Rodeo crowd, Gallup, 1987
33. Bull dogging, Gallup, 1981
34. Barrel racing, Gallup, 1987
35. Behind the chutes, Gallup, 1987
36. Behind the chutes, Gallup, 1981
37. Behind the bar, Holbrook, 1980
38. Prairie Moon lady, Winslow, 1982
39. Prairie Moon ladies, Winslow, 1982
40. Jasper, Proprietor, Prairie Moon Tavern, Winslow, 1981
41. Palomino Bar, Gallup, 1986
42. Jerry Franklin and the Navajo Midnighters, Milan's Club, Gallup, 1981
43. Milan's Club, Gallup, 1981
44. Rosetree Bar, Flagstaff, 1980
45. Inside the Commercial Club, Gallup, 1986
46. Inside the American Bar, Gallup, 1987
47. Farmington, New Mexico, 1982
48. Holbrook, 1980
49. Air fresheners, Gallup, 1986
50. Stealing his boots, Flagstaff, 1980
51. Tall ones for the road, Gallup, 1986
52. Passed out in the truck, Gallup, 1986
53. "Hey guys, come over here," Winslow, 1986
54. But he likes to sleep there, Gallup, 1986
55. Gallup, 1987
56. Gallup, 1983
57. Gallup, 1981
58. Gallup, 1981
59. Cut them out, Holbrook, 1984
60. Wrong way on the freeway, near Fort Wingate, 1985
61. Wrong way on the highway, Gallup, 1982

62. Run over by a drunk, Gallup, 1981
63. In the body bag, Gallup, 1981
64. Run over by a train, Flagstaff, 1982
65. They cannot save the baby, Farmington, 1985
66. Hit the car head on, Gray Mountain, 1983
67. The little girl is gone, Gray Mountain, 1983
68. Body outline, blood and a quarter, Gray Mountain, 1980
69. Looking for trouble, Gallup, 1986
70. Randy, Gallup, 1986
71. He wears a top hat, Gallup, 1985
72. Waiting, Gallup, 1986
73. "No pictures, no pictures!" Gallup, 1986
74. "Tell us what happened," Gallup, 1982
75. Donna, Gallup, 1984
76. Inspection day, Gallup, 1987
77. Time to get out, Gallup, 1986
78. "Like hell you'll get me in that cell!" Gallup, 1987
79. He is trying to pick the lock, Gallup, 1987
80. In the side pocket, Gallup, 1986
81. The small tank, Gallup, 1986
82. The big tank, Gallup, 1982
83. Fight! Gallup, 1986
84. Checking her eyes, Flagstaff, 1980
85. Hit in the face with a pool cue, Club 66, Flagstaff, 1980
86. He just shakes, Gallup, 1986
87. Dying words, Flagstaff, 1980
88. Stabbed in the chest, Gallup, 1986
89. Slashed across the face, Commercial Club, Gallup, 1982
90. He may not make it, Gallup, 1987
91. "They took my money," Gallup, 1986
92. "And my money too," Gallup, 1986
93. "They took everything I had," Gallup, 1986
94. "They cleaned me out," Gallup, 1986
95. He is going to jump, Indian Hospital, Gallup, 1987
96. "One step closer and I'll jump!" Indian Hospital, Gallup, 1987
97. Veteran's Cemetery, Window Rock, 1987
98. El Presidente, looking, Gallup, 1986

Epilogue

Dialogue between tourist couple
and Gallup Police Lieutenant

Recorded conversation (abridged) between a responding
Gallup Police Lieutenant and a traveling couple
as they depart the Sahara Motel, Gallup, New Mexico
3 A.M. - August 15, 1987

Lt.:	"Good morning, how can I help you sir? I'm the night supervisor."
Wife:	"You can't."
Lt.:	"What's the problem?"
Husband:	"The whole night has been a terrible disaster. You've got people out here fighting . . ."
Wife:	(interrupting) "Do you want to see the blood?"
Husband:	"Honey, shut up! Officer, there are people around here getting into cars drunk, staggering drunk . . ."
Wife:	(interrupting) "Honey, show them the blood!"

Lt.: "We are having trouble all over town. It's Ceremonial and there are a lot of people in town."

Wife: "We've been driving from East St. Louis today. We come and check in and want to get some sleep. What do we get? We get hassle, after hassle, after hassle. Here we are trying to get some sleep — cars peal out, drunks everywhere — fight, after fight, after fight. This town isn't civilized. Give me a fucking break!"

Lt.: "We do the best we can. With only eight officers on the street, we've put over five hundred people in jail and answered seventy-one calls tonight."

Wife: "Don't you have any laws here? We've been all over the world and I've never, never dealt with anything like this."

Husband: "That's true. It would be easier to name the places I haven't been, and I have never run into shit like this. Even California has better laws than this, and hey, that's a wild assed state, let's face it. Honey, did you get my shirt?"

Wife: "Yeah, I did."

Husband: "Thank you, pumpkin."

Wife: "I'll tell you what, we aren't the only ones to call your police department. We've talked to several others that have. I've never dealt with anything like this."

Lt.: "As I've said, we've been handling a lot of calls. There are always a lot of calls at Ceremonial. Sorry you feel that way Mam."

Wife: (loading car) "Well, I'll tell you, I can't wait to come back to Gallup, New Mexico. You're sorry — we are the ones who haven't slept since East St. Louis this morning, and we're going to get the hell out of your goddamn town — because you can't control your town."

Wife: (getting into car) "I've lived in Arizona, I've lived in Michigan, I've lived in Massachusetts, I've lived in Minnesota, I've lived in California, and I've never, never seen anything like this! Don't the laws of the United States apply here?"

Wife: (driving off) "Have a nice night."

Lt.: "Good night."

Printing
FABE LITHOGRAPHY
Tucson, Arizona
Stanley Fabe

Photolithography
Mickey Delfiner

Press
Skip Bogel
Arturo Durazo

Plates
Douglas Peterson

Film Stripping
Merle Davis

Binding
ROSWELL BOOKBINDING
Phoenix, Arizona
Michael Roswell
Martha Reed

Typesetting
MORNEAU TYPOGRAPHERS
Phoenix, Arizona

Book Design
Mark Sanders
Phoenix, Arizona